This book belongs to:

_____

_____

_____

_____

Agnes Green
Visit my website at www.apriltalebooks.com

Printed in the United States of America
First Printing: August 2019

www.apriltalebooks.com

Agnes Green

Tucked in the Barn

Illustrator Natalia Vetrova

At home on the farm,
you so love the barn.
With your animal friends,
so many days you will spend.

But sweet child of mine,
now is the time,
to lay your head
on your cozy bed.

The sun is low
so it's time to go.
The animals are asleep,
and we don't hear a peep.

Night is slowly falling
and Daddy is calling.
We've said goodnight.
Let's close the barn tight.

But mama, no!
I don't want to go,
for here I'll sleep,
snuggled in with the sheep.

Tucked in the barn,
cozy, safe and warm—
with the lambs, I'll stay,
curled up where they lay.

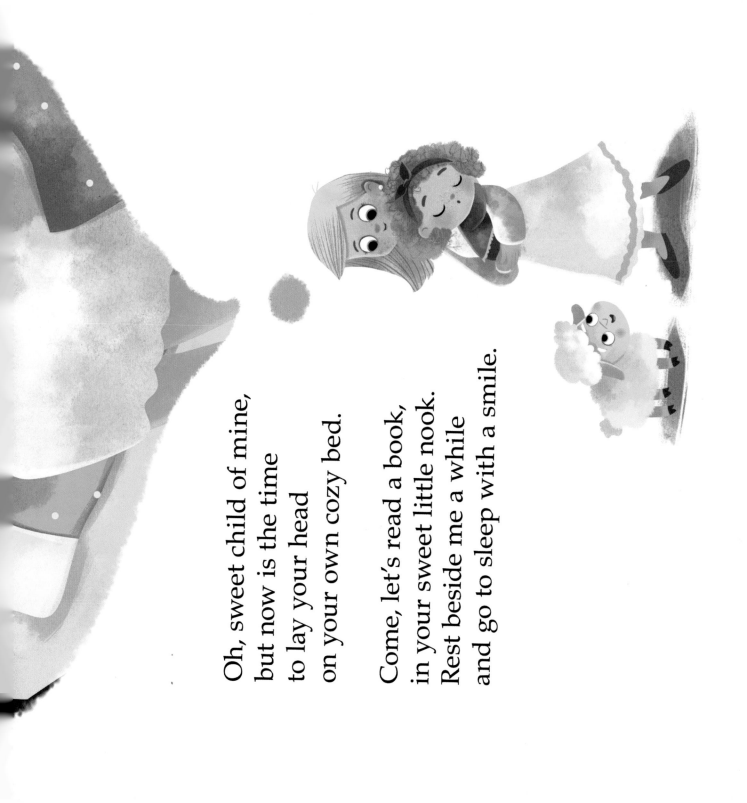

Oh, sweet child of mine,
but now is the time
to lay your head
on your own cozy bed.

Come, let's read a book,
in your sweet little nook.
Rest beside me a while
and go to sleep with a smile.

But mama, no!
I don't want to go.
I'll stay here for now
beside this snoring cow.

Tucked in the barn,
cozy, safe and warm
on their soft bed of hay
with the calves... I'm okay.

Oh, sweet child of mine,
but now is the time
to lay your head
on your own little bed.

Come, I'll rub your back,
after you've finished your snack.
Inside you'll be warm
but you'll be cold in the barn.

But mama, no!
I don't want to go.
I'll sleep till sun-up
out here with the pup.

Tucked in the barn,
cozy, safe and warm
with the puppies, I'll cuddle.
On their blanket, we'll huddle.

Oh, sweet child of mine,
but now is the time
to lay your head
on your own warm bed.

Come inside now, you hear?
It's getting dark out, I fear.
Daddy's waiting for us,
so please don't make a fuss.

But mama, no!
I don't want to go.
I'll curl up in this pen
and wake with the hens.

Tucked in the barn,
cozy, safe and warm
with the chicks, I will nest,
in their coop for a rest.

Oh, sweet child of mine,
but now is the time
to lay your head
on your own soft bed.

Come, I'll sing you a song,
and you'll be asleep before long.
Your room is all ready,
and your eyes are so heavy.

But mama no,
I don't want to go.
I'll lie with the rabbits:
their hutch, I'll inhabit.

Tucked in the barn,
cozy, safe and warm
with the bunnies, I'll doze,
feeling soft fur on my nose.

Come close your eyes,
I've got a surprise.
Here in your bed,
is a treat like I said.

Oh, sweet child of mine,
but now is the time
to lay your head
on your own lovely bed.

All lined up in a row
are the stuffed animals you know.
With these toys you can sleep:
a cow, dog, hen, bunny and sheep.

Come lay your head
and curl up in your bed.
In your sweet dreams,
so real they will seem.

Tomorrow we will go,
Outside. You know,
soon it will be morning,
the sun'll be up without warning.

And when you wake up,
you can go see that pup,
say hello to the sheep,
and hear the chicks peep.

You can cuddle a bunny;
they're so soft and funny.
Then you can go hug the cow,
but it's time to sleep now.

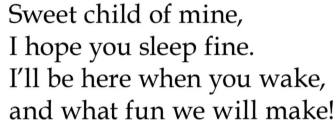

Sweet child of mine,
I hope you sleep fine.
I'll be here when you wake,
and what fun we will make!

Thank you for reading!
I hope you enjoyed
this cute little story!

Reviews from awesome customers
like you help others to feel confident
about choosing this book too.

Please take a minute to review it
and share your experience!

Thank you in advance
for helping me out!
I will be forever grateful.

Yours, Agnes Green

"It's time for bed... Hip hip hooray! Let's all give a cheer!
The day is through. We've had such fun. Now sleepy time draws near.

Before you drift away to dream, let's check in at the zoo.
I hear they're having a parade and a pajama party too!"

Made in the USA
Lexington, KY
08 November 2019

Don't miss another book of mine!
"Today I'm a Monster"